GO SHOW the WORLD

A Celebration of Indigenous Heroes

BY WAB KINEW

PICTURES BY
JOE MORSE

tundra

There's a power in these lands,
one that's been here many years,
strong enough to make you stand
and forget all of your fears.
It started in the past with a blast of light and thunder;
ancient ones looked up and beheld the sky with wonder.

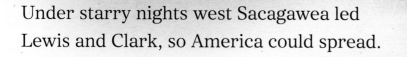

Under starry nights west Sacagawea led
Lewis and Clark, so America could spread.

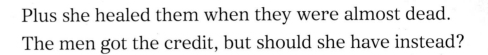

Plus she healed them when they were almost dead.
The men got the credit, but should she have instead?

Before he made the big leagues or won Olympic Gold
little Jim Thorpe ran all the time, I'm told.
His twin died at boarding school, leaving Jim alone.
All he knew to do was run,
so ran the whole way home.

Finally his dad said, Jim, don't run away.
No matter how far you run, Brother's gone to stay.

It might be tough now but you will be something.
Before you leave, my son, I wanna tell you one thing . . .

You're a person who matters.
Yes, it's true.
Now go show the world what a person who matters can do.

Sue LaFlesche Picotte pushed doors
'til they let her in.
They may have called her "too dark"
or even "too feminine,"
but she kept working hard
even as they mocked her,
'til she earned a name that stuck . . .
Now they call her Doctor.

In a foster home
Beatrice's heart reigned free.
Wrote a book about her life
and called it *April Raintree*.

You need to stand strong;
be Pegahmagabow,
who fought for freedom abroad
and right here at home.

When you feel tired,
remember Te-Wau-Zee clear.
She walked a sad trail
but shed no tear,

carried sweat rocks the whole way
so culture could live.
   When they asked her why she did what she did
      she simply said,

You are people who matter.

Yes, it's true.

Now go show the world what people who matter can do.

These, a few of my heroes,
maybe now your heroes too.
Let's look ahead at our lives,
think of what we want to do.

Maybe be a doctor
or movie star, it might happen.
Maybe we do both,
like our friend, Evan Adams.

We're like John Herrington —
in space, no wait, Mars.
We're like Carey Price standing
tall against a charge.

Like Waneek Horn-Miller —
hurt, but keep right on.
Become captain of our country —
our spirit's too strong.

Tecumseh said, perfect your life;
make it serve the people.

Crazy Horse lived free,
his spirit like an eagle.

Net-no-kwa was a woman,
like most, a true warrior.
Strong and independent, fierce
as any man before her.

Remember, always do right.
Try to be positive.
If you ever do wrong,
make it up, and please forgive.
All paths are open to you,
the brave, you take a stand.
Wherever you go,
these words echo through the land:

We are people who matter.
Yes, it's true.
Now let's show the world what people who matter can do.

AUTHOR'S NOTE

Indigenous peoples and cultures have shaped our history and world, whether through the actions of great leaders, like the people included in this book, or by naming the places we live, like Seattle, Chicago, Toronto and Canada. This highlights a simple truth: Whether or not you have Indigenous blood, if you live in North America today, some part of your identity has an Indigenous character. I hope that learning about some Indigenous heroes will help you better understand the original peoples of these lands, their descendants and even yourself.

I was inspired in the writing of this book by Barack Obama's wonderful picture book, *Of Thee I Sing: A Letter to My Daughters*, which I love reading to my sons as it features the president highlighting some of his favorite heroes. I was also inspired by K'naan's song "Take a Minute," in which he spends a few lines praising his idols, including Nelson Mandela and Mahatma Gandhi. That led me to write a remix of his song highlighting heroes from the Indigenous community, which I called "Heroes."

When I was thinking about writing a book for children, I knew that I wanted to take elements from each of these influences and create a new song to celebrate some great leaders from Indigenous communities.

Too few people know who these leaders are, even though they have done such amazing things. All these people believed in themselves. Coming from a community where too many young people struggle to find success, I strongly believe it's important for every young person to hear the words "you're a person who matters" so they can learn to believe in themselves too.

As we grapple with some of the big challenges of our day, from global warming to inequality, and work toward solutions, I know that Indigenous peoples and cultures have something to offer. People who grow up hearing that the Earth is our mother and that water is life must have something valuable to say about sustainability. And those who are taught from birth that we are all related must have something important to contribute to our shared quest for justice.

Joe Morse has captured these values beautifully in his art. The images he has created weave the cultures, spiritualities and individual personalities of our heroes into a wonderful tapestry that connects them to their place here on Earth, but also to each of us.

We walk on the same lands as the heroes celebrated in this book. I hope their examples can help each of us, big and small, relearn that the lands are sacred and we ought to respect them. I also hope their stories of triumph over adversity inspire each of us to reach our full potential.

BIOGRAPHIES

SACAGAWEA (1788–1812) was a Shoshone woman who acted as a guide, advisor and negotiator for the American travelers Lewis and Clark on their expedition. She carried her newborn baby along on the journey and connected Indigenous peoples and knowledge with a growing America.

JIM THORPE (1887–1953) was a Sac and Fox man who was voted the Greatest Athlete of the first fifty years of the twentieth century by the Associated Press. He was an Olympic Gold Medal–winning pentathlete and decathlete, pro football player, pro basketball player and pro baseball player.

DR. SUSAN LAFLESCHE PICOTTE (1865–1915) was an Omaha woman who was one of the first Indigenous physicians at a time when even being a female doctor was uncommon. She traveled to Victorian women's societies to raise money for her medical education, then returned home to improve the health of her people.

FRANCIS PEGAHMAGABOW (1889–1952) was an Anishinaabe soldier who was the most highly decorated First Nations soldier in Canadian military history; he is said to have been the most effective sniper of World War I. He returned home and became chief of Wasauksing First Nation, fighting for his people's civil rights in Canada. As Brian D. McInnes wrote in his book, *Sounding Thunder*, Pegahmagabow once translated his family name as "it advances and halts, advances and halts," which was derived from his great-great-grandfather Bebagamigaabaw (hence the line "Be Pegahmagabow").

BEATRICE CULLETON MOSIONIER (1949–PRESENT) is a Métis author from Canada who courageously wrote the seminal novel *In Search of April Raintree* in 1983. It is based in part on her own experiences growing up in foster care and helped many to begin understanding issues in the child welfare system and of missing and murdered Indigenous women and girls.

TE-WAU-ZEE (AROUND 1879), whose name means Yellow Buffalo Woman, was the matriarch of the Camp family of the Ponca Nation who were forcibly relocated in 1879 to their present-day home in Oklahoma. She was told by the soldiers she could only bring what she could carry, so she hid four sweat lodge rocks in her belongings and walked hundreds of miles with them. She did this so her descendants would still be able to practice their culture. The Camp family still proudly practices the Ponca culture and goes to sweat lodges today.

DR. EVAN ADAMS (1966–PRESENT) is a Two Spirit physician and public health official from Sliammon First Nation in British Columbia, Canada. He is also a well-respected actor who has appeared in movies like *Smoke Signals* and many theater productions. Today he works as the chief medical officer for the B.C. First Nations Health Authority.

JOHN HERRINGTON (1958–PRESENT) is a Chickasaw man who became the first Native American to fly in space. On his thirteen-day mission in 2002 he brought with him the official flag of the Chickasaw Nation and completed three space walks. He wrote a book about his experience called *Misson to Space*, which includes both English and Chickasaw words. He is also a retired U.S. Naval Pilot.

CAREY PRICE (1987–PRESENT) is an NHL goalie and member of the Ulkatcho First Nation. He has won many NHL awards, including both the Vezina Trophy for top goaltender of the year and the Hart Trophy for NHL MVP. In 2014, he helped Canada win a gold medal in Ice Hockey at the Winter Olympics, where he was also named the tournament's top goaltender.

WANEEK HORN-MILLER (1975–PRESENT) is a Mohawk woman who was stabbed by an army soldier's bayonet when she was fourteen during the Oka crisis in Quebec. In spite of this, she represented Team Canada as captain of the water polo team at the 2000 Olympics and won a gold medal at the 1999 Pan Am games.

TECUMSEH (1768–1813) was a Shawnee leader who unified dozens of nations to defend their homelands and way of life. He helped defend what is now called Canada from invasion during the first year of the War of 1812. His words are still quoted as inspiration by soldiers and warriors to this day.

CRAZY HORSE (1842–1877), or Thašúŋke Witkó in his native tongue, was an Oglala Lakota war chief who participated in many battles during his career. He scored one of the biggest Indigenous victories ever by defeating the U.S. Cavalry at the Battle of Little Big Horn in 1876. As a young man, he had a vision in which he was taught to paint his face with a lightning bolt for protection while fighting.

NET-NO-KWA (AROUND 1750) was an Odawa woman who was a spiritual and political leader and chief of her clan. She adopted a non-Indigenous boy named John Tanner and raised him as her own. He chose to stay with Net-no-kwa's people as an adult and wrote about their way of life.

For Dom, Bezh & Baby . . .
because every kid needs a hero **W K**

In memory of my sister Virg **J M**

Text copyright © 2018 by Wab Kinew
Illustrations copyright © 2018 by Joe Morse

Tundra Books, an imprint of Penguin Random House Canada Young Readers, a Penguin Random House Company

Library and Archives Canada Cataloguing in Publication

Kinew, Wab, 1981-, author
        Go show the world : a celebration of Indigenous heroes / by Wab Kinew; illustrated by Joe Morse.

Issued in print and electronic formats.
ISBN 978-0-7352-6292-8 (hardcover).--ISBN 978-0-7352-6293-5 (EPUB)

        1. Indians of North America--Biography--Juvenile literature. I. Morse,
Joe, 1960-, illustrator II. Title.

E89.K55 2018   j970.004'9700922   C2017-905566-6
                                                          C2017-905567-4

Published simultaneously in the United States of America by Tundra Books of Northern New York, an imprint of Penguin Random House Canada Young Readers, a Penguin Random House Company

Library of Congress Control Number: 2017951211

Edited by Jessica Burgess and Lynne Missen
Designed by Lisa Jager
The artwork in this book was created with watercolor and digital color and collage.
The text was set in Core Serif.

Printed and bound in China

www.penguinrandomhouse.ca

1   2   3   4   5   22   21   20   19   18

Penguin
Random House
TUNDRA BOOKS